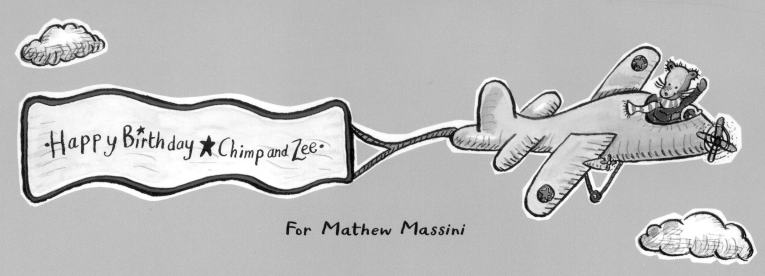

For Mathew Massini

Meet Chimp and Zee on the Anholt website at www.anholt.co.uk

Happy Birthday Chimp and Zee copyright © Frances Lincoln Limited 2005
Text copyright © Laurence Anholt 2005
Illustrations copyright © Catherine Anholt 2005

The right of Laurence Anholt to be identified as the Author
and of Catherine Anholt to be identified as the Illustrator
of this work has been asserted by them in accordance
with the Copyright, Designs and Patents Act, 1988.

First published in Great Britain in 2005 and in the USA in 2006 by
Frances Lincoln Children's Books, 4 Torriano Mews, Torriano Avenue, London NW5 2RZ
www.franceslincoln.com

Distributed in the USA by Publishers Group West

British Library Cataloguing in Publication Data available on request

ISBN 1-84507-507-2

Set in Chimp and Zee
Designed by Sarah Massini

Printed in China
1 3 5 7 9 10 8 6 4 2

Happy Birthday
Chimp and Zee

Please come to
Chimp and Zee's Party

☐ No, I can't come.

☑ YES, I CAN COME.

CATHERINE AND
LAURENCE ANHOLT

FRANCES LINCOLN CHILDREN'S BOOKS

This is Chimp, this is Zee,
on a birthday morning in the coconut tree.

Mumkey sits up in bed.
"Goodness!" she says. "Whatever is all
that noise? The whole house is shaking."

It is
Chimp and Zee
going bananas.

Ha, ha, ha!
Hee, hee, hee!
Happy birthday,
Chimp and Zee!

Someone is calling from outside...
"Special delivery for two birthday chimps!" calls the mailman.

Quick, quick, quick!
Down the ladder and
into the birthday morning.

Chimp pulls this way,
Zee pulls that way,
and inside are...

Here is Papakey with two more surprises.

Chimp pulls this way,
Zee pulls that way,
and inside are...

two birthday scooters,
with two birthday tooters!

Toot, toot, toot!
Tee, hee, hee!
Can't catch Chimp!
Can't catch Zee!

"Now, come close so I can whisper," says Papakey. "There is one more surprise that is the biggest, most enormous, stripiest Birthday Surprise of all."

Chimp and Zee's eyes grow as big as birthday balloons.

"It is waiting for you right in the middle of Jungletown."

Toot, toot, toot!
Tee, hee, hee!
"AWAY WE GO!"
shout Chimp and Zee.

"Wait for us!" calls Mumkey.

Everybody is going
to Jungletown today.
The jungle path is very busy.

"HAPPY BIRTHDAY!"

shout all their friends.

Toot, toot, toot!
Tee, hee, hee!
Follow Chimp!
Follow Zee!

Off to Jungletown
to find the Stripy Surprise!

"Hold tight!" calls Papakey. "We're going uphill."

Higher, higher, higher until they reach the top.

And there is Jungletown far below.
Chimp and Zee can see something amazing.
They are more excited than ever.
It looks like an enormous Stripy Surprise!

"Now then," says Mumkey,
"the path is steep, so you must stay close
and you must not rush away."

But Chimp and Zee do NOT stay close.
They DO rush away.
"Come back! Come back!" calls everybody.

Chimp and Zee take a short cut through the Slimy Swamp.

"Wherever are those birthday twins?"
cry Mumkey and Papakey.

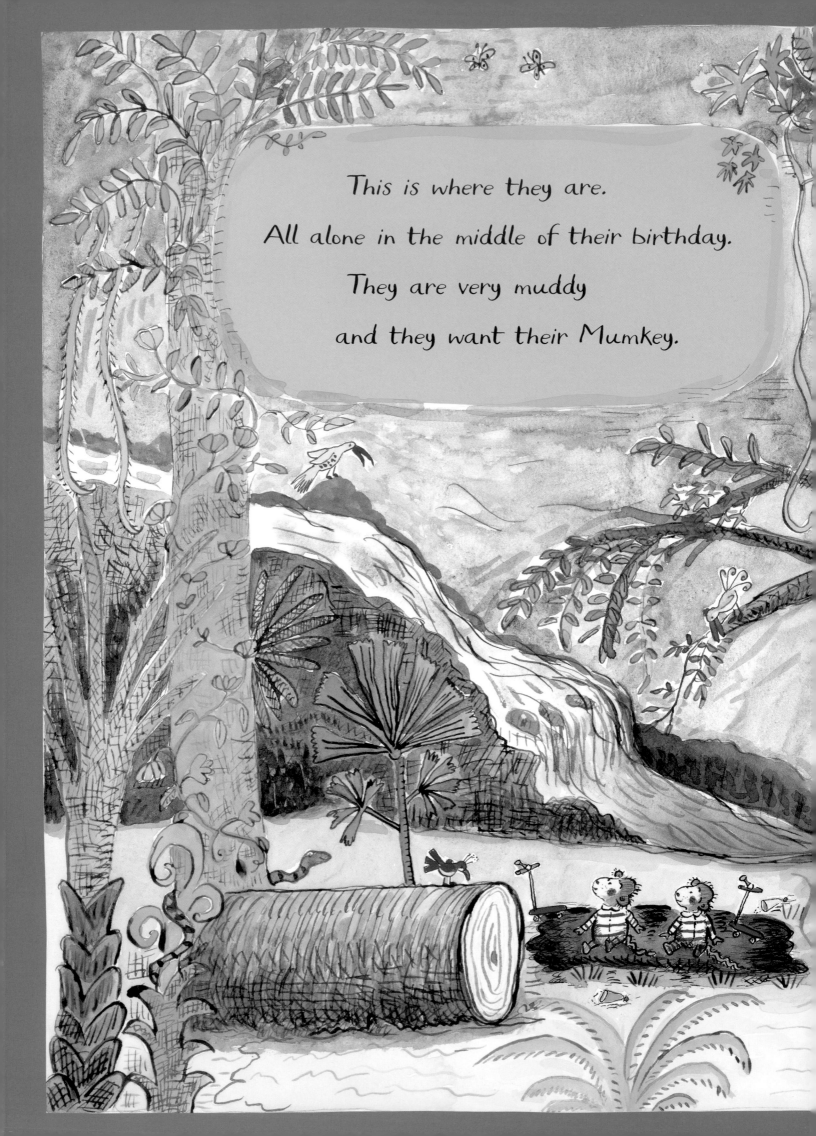

This is where they are.

All alone in the middle of their birthday.

They are very muddy

and they want their Mumkey.

"Puff, puff, PUFF!"
Something is coming through
the Slimy Swamp.
But it is NOT Mumkey!

It is a Big Green Thing with a tail like a dragon;
and a fiery mouth – even more like a dragon!

"Boo, hoo, hoo!
Wee, wee, wee!
We want Mumkey,"
squeal Chimp and Zee.

This is NOT a nice
birthday surprise.

Then Chimp remembers the tooters on the scooters...
TOOT! TOOT! TOOT! The dragon turns and runs away.

Here are Mumkey and Papakey
racing through the swamp.
"There you are, birthday boo-boos!"

Together they walk into the middle of Jungletown.
Where has everyone gone?

And HERE is...
the biggest,
most enormous,
most colorful,
most amazing,
most wonderful,
stripiest surprise in
the whole wide Jungletown.

Whatever can it be?

a birthday tea for Chimp and Zee!

Chimp pulls this way,

Zee pulls that way,

and inside is...

Only one person is late for the party.
"Here she comes now," says Mumkey.

"Puff, puff, PUFF!"

Who can it be?

A Big Green Thing with a tail at the back
and a HUGE BIRTHDAY CAKE at the front!

Then everybody sings...

"Ha, ha, ha!
Hee, hee, hee!
Happy birthday,
Chimp and Zee!"

And Chimp and Zee
and all their friends go
ABSOLUTELY BANANAS!

The birthday moon sails high over Jungletown.

Chimp and Zee have one last surprise for each other.

Chimp pulls this way,
Zee pulls that way,
and inside are...

two very squashy
birthday bananas!

"Love from you
and love from me.
Twins together,"
say Chimp and Zee.